Momotaro

Long ago in Japan
lived an old woodcutter and his wife.
They had no children,
and sometimes they were very lonely.

One day, the old woman was down
by the river when she saw a large peach
floating toward her. She snatched it up
and took it home to show her husband.

Suddenly, the peach broke open.
There, in the middle, was a tiny baby boy!
The old man and woman were very excited.

"At last we have a child to love
and care for," they cried.
"We shall call him Momotaro."

In the middle of the river, not far from
the old couple's village, was an island.
On the island lived a fierce band of ogres.

Sometimes, at night, the ogres
would raid the village looking for treasure.
Everyone was terrified of the ogres.

One day, when Momotaro
had grown into a big, strong boy,
he said to his parents,
"I am going to fight the ogres
until they give back all the treasure
they have stolen."

The old man and woman
were afraid for their son,
but they were proud of him, too.

"Here," said the old woman.
"Take these three dumplings
for your journey.
Please be careful."

Momotaro hugged his parents
and went on his way.

As Momotaro was walking, he met a monkey.
"Where are you going?" asked the monkey.

"I'm going to fight the ogres and get back our
treasure," said Momotaro. "Who are you?"

10

"I am the cleverest monkey
in the world, and I will come too
if you give me a dumpling,"
said the monkey.

Momotaro gave the monkey a dumpling,
and they walked on together
until they met a pheasant.

"Where are you going?"
asked the pheasant.

"We are going to fight the ogres,"
said Momotaro. "Who are you?"

"I am the strongest pheasant in the world,
and I will come too if you give me
a dumpling," said the pheasant.

Momotaro gave the pheasant a dumpling,
and the three of them walked on together
until they met a dog.

"Where are you going?"
asked the dog.

"We are going to fight the ogres,"
said Momotaro. "Who are you?"

"I am the fiercest dog in the world,
and I will come too if you give me
a dumpling," said the dog.

15

Momotaro gave the dog his last dumpling,
and the four of them walked on
until they saw the ogres' island.

"How can we cross the river?"
asked Momotaro.

"No problem," said the pheasant.
"Just hop on my back,
and I'll fly you across."

"I can swim across," said the dog,
"and the monkey can ride on my back."

The four friends landed safely on the island.
"There is the ogres' castle," said Momotaro.
"But how can we get inside?"

"No problem," said the monkey,
and he scampered over the wall
and unlocked the door.

Momotaro and his friends
stormed inside the castle.
The attack took the ogres by surprise.

The monkey tripped the ogres up
while the dog nipped their ankles
and the pheasant flew at their faces.

The ogres were so afraid, they ran away.
Only the ogre king stayed to face Momotaro.

"Please take pity on us," he begged.
"If you let us live, we will give you
all our treasure."

"Only if you promise never to steal
from my village again," said Momotaro.

The ogre agreed, and soon Momotaro
and his friends were back in the village
with all the stolen treasure.

Everyone in the village was overjoyed to see
their hero return with all the treasure.

"Momotaro," said his parents,
"you are truly the bravest boy in the world."

"I don't know about brave," answered
Momotaro, "but I was lucky to have
such wonderful friends to help me.
Without my friends,
I could never have beaten the ogres."